for BUTTERWORTH
ki...

BLOOMSBURY
CHILDREN'S
BOOKS

First published in Great Britain in 2004
by Bloomsbury Publishing Plc
38 Soho Square, London, W1D 3HB

This paperback edition first published in 2005

Text and Illustrations copyright © Ross Collins 2004
The moral right of the author/illustrator has been asserted

A CIP catalogue record of this book is available from the British Library

ISBN 0 7475 7142 2

Printed in Hong Kong/China

1 3 5 7 9 10 8 6 4 2

All papers used by Bloomsbury Publishing are natural, recyclable products
made from wood grown in well-managed forests. The manufacturing processes
conform to the environmental regulations of the country of origin.

www.bloomsbury.com/germs

Germs

Ross Collins

BLOOMSBURY
CHILDREN'S
BOOKS

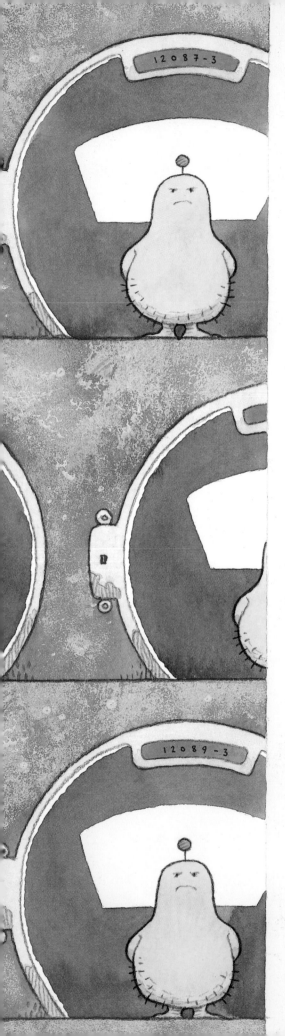

Pox heard *the* Matron
coming before she arrived.

"Incubating time's up,
Chickenpox 12087-2!" she yelled.
"Time you learned how to germ proper!"

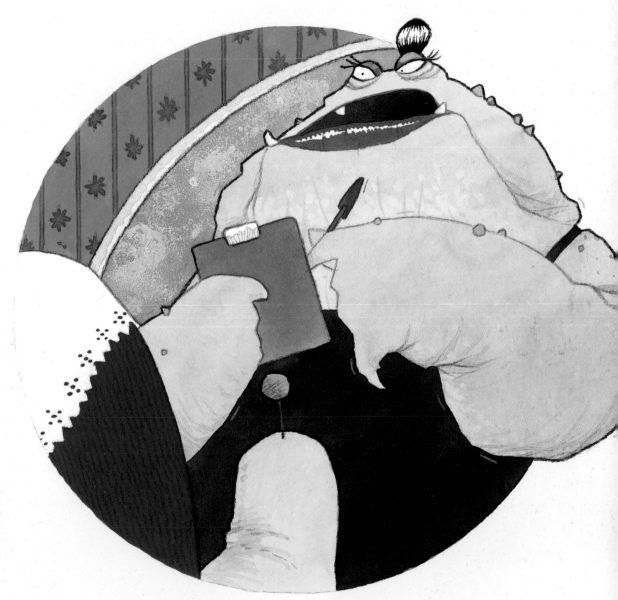

"My friends call me Pox," smiled Pox.

"I'm not your friend," snarled Matron.
"Now pack your bags!"

Later that morning the Bubonic Bus
arrived to take Pox and the other cadets
to Germ Academy – where minor infections
are turned into real germs.

Once Pox had passed his
medical to prove that he was unhealthy,

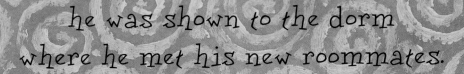

he was shown to the dorm
where he met his new roommates.

After lights out the other germs gathered round Pox to tell stories.
Each boasted of a terrible outbreak which a relative had started.

"But didn't it make the children miserable?" asked Pox.
"That's the point, you numpty," sneered Scab.
But Pox didn't get it.

For the next week Pox came bottom of the class in everything.

Medicine Self-Defence

Flight School

All too soon Pox was assigned his first mission.
"But she looks so sweet," said Pox.
"Make 'er ill," growled Pus.

That night Pox was airdropped outside Myrtle's house and managed to remember enough of his flight training to glide successfully up her left nostril.

Pox slumped against a vein and sulked.
"This job stinks," he thought. "What right have I to..."
But then he heard a noise, getting louder and louder
and heading right for him...

Before he could hide he was surrounded.
It was Myrtle's Immune System
and *they* didn't look friendly.

"There he is!" shouted one.
"You picked the wrong kid to infect!" yelled another.

Meanwhile back at Germ Central alarms began to ring.
"The target isn't showing signs of infection!"
barked Commander Phlegm.
"Chickenpox 12087-2 has loused up his mission!"

"Let us go in, sir!"
    sneered Pox's roommates.
"We'll give 'er a birthday
    she'll never forget, sir!"
"My brave boys," hacked the Commander.

Pox was in trouble.

The Immune System was trained to pulverize little germs like him.

"Wait!" he shouted, "I'm on your side!"

"Oh yeah – and I'm a fungal infection," mocked a voice at the back.

"Why should we trust YOU, germ boy?" scowled another.

"Because four big ugly germs will be coming soon," said Pox, "and without my help Myrtle could be ill in bed for weeks."

The army paused.

"OK," they said. "What do we do?"

Pox drew up
a plan.

With seconds to spare Pox gave the command and a startled Myrtle let rip the biggest sneeze of her life.

FIRE!

Achoooooo

Dazed and confused, the germs woke up a minute later.
Rash looked around. "Look," he said. "We made it, we're in!"

They all cheered.
"Let's go infect little girl!" cried Pus.

They all cheered again.
"What's that noise coming down the tunnel?" asked Scab.

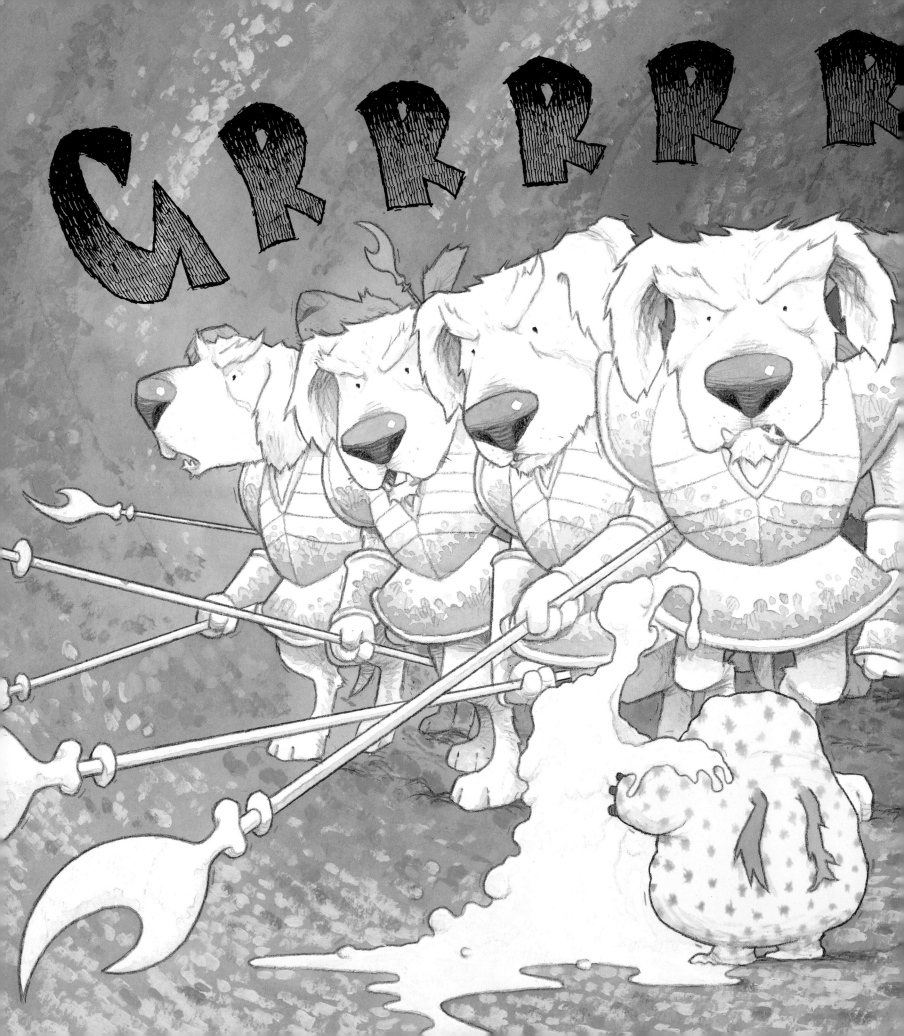

"I don't think we're in Myrtle," gulped Snot.

"Three cheers for Pox!" cried the Immune System.

Pox was hoisted up on shoulders and taken on a triumphant tour of Myrtle where crowds of cells cheered the germ who had saved them all.

"We've never met a heroic germ before," they said.

"Neither have I," said Pox.

"What can we ever do to repay you?"

"Well," said Pox, "I do rather need a place to stay..."

Thanks to his germ knowledge Pox was made Honorary Chief of the Immune System. As for Myrtle, haven't you heard?

Well, she became...

But that's another story.

How do germs get in us?

Germs can fly into us from a cough or a sneeze. Or they can be spread by mucky fingers or sharing a sticky sandwich.

How do our bodies fight germs?

Over squillions of years our bodies have worked out how to fight off lots of common germs like Snot and Rash. When they arrive, our Immune System jumps on them until we are well again.

How do we help our bodies to stay healthy?

We can eat good food and run about to stay healthy. Doctors can help us too with vaccinations and icky medicines.

Remember - not all germs are nasty. Some of us actually help you lot out - just ask Myrtle